A Note to Parents and Teachers

The *Dorling Kindersley Readers* series is a compelling reading program designed in conjunction with leading literacy experts, including Dr. Linda Gambrell, director of the School of Education at Clemson University. Dr. Gambrell has served on the board of directors of the International Reading Association and as president of the National Reading Conference.

The series combines a highly visual approach with engaging, easy-to-read text. Each reader is guaranteed to capture a child's interest while developing his or her reading skills, general knowledge, and love of reading.

The four levels of readers are aimed at different reading abilities, enabling you to choose the books that are exactly right for your children:

Level 1—Beginning to Read
Level 2—Beginning to Read Alone
Level 3—Reading Alone
Level 4—Proficient Readers

The "normal" age at which a child begins to read can be anywhere from three to eight years old, so these levels are intended only as a general guideline.

No matter which level you select, you can be sure that you are helping your child learn to read, then read to learn!

Dorling DK Kindersley

LONDON, NEW YORK, SYDNEY, DELHI, PARIS,
MUNICH, and JOHANNESBURG

Senior Editor Cynthia O'Neill
Editor Rebecca Knowles
Senior Managing Art Editor Cathy Tincknell
Publishimg Manager Karen Dolan
Senior DTP Designer Andrew O'Brien
Production Nicola Torode
US Editor Gary Werner
Reading Consultant Linda Gambrell, PhD

First American Edition, 2000

00 01 02 03 04 05 10 9 8 7 6 5 4 3 2 1

Published in the United States by
Dorling Kindersley Publishing, Inc.
95 Madison Avenue
New York, New York 10016

Library of Congress Cataloging-in-Publication Data
Teitelbaum, Michael
  Feel the Sting! / by Michael Teitelbaum.
    p. cm. -- (Dorling Kindersley readers)
  ISBN 0-7894-6674-0 (HC) -- ISBN 0-7894-6760-7 (pbk.)
  1. Sting (Wrestler), 1959---Juvenile literature. 2.
Wrestlers--United States--Biography--Juvenile literature. [1. Sting
(Wrestler), 1959- 2. Wrestlers.]   I. Title. II. Series.
  GV1196.S75 T45 2000
  796.812'092--dc21

          00-034052

Printed and bound in the United States.

Illustrations by Paul Trevillion.
The publisher would like to thank the following for
their kind permission to reproduce their images:
Ronald Grant Archive: 44cl.
Special photography by Dave King
All other photographic images provided by World
Championship Wrestling, Inc.
Special thanks to Joseph Lester, WCW, Inc.

see our complete catalog at
www.dk.com

Contents

DORLING KINDERSLEY *READERS*

FEEL THE
STING

Written by Michael Teitelbaum

PROFICIENT
4
READERS

A Dorling Kindersley Book

Thrill-seeker
Outside the ring, Sting rides motorcycles and drives off-road vehicles—as if he doesn't get enough excitement at work!

Free time
Sting is always active, even out of the ring. He enjoys waterskiing, golf, and fixing up his old house.

Beginnings

High above the arena, a dark figure moves silently among the rafters. At last, someone in the crowd looks up and spots him.

Whispers spread through the arena. "He's here! He's back!" people cry. Sting, the mysterious warrior of WCW, is in the house!

His appearance may have changed over the years, but Sting has always been one of the most extraordinary figures in wrestling. Where did this fascinating character, who keeps both his fans and his opponents off-balance, come from?

Sting was born Steven James Borden, in Omaha, Nebraska, and grew up in Santa Clara, California. As a child and teenager, Sting made the most of the warm California climate and was an excellent athlete.

Surprisingly, though, he didn't wrestle in high school or college.

California dreamin'
Sting has played volleyball on the California beaches since he was a teenager.

Sting played basketball. He was the star player on his high school team. He was so energetic and agile that he played his opponents right off the court.

At College of the Canyons, a junior college in California, Sting was a power forward on the basketball team. His impressive jumping ability, which later shaped his wrestling style, helped him pull down rebounds and slam dunk the ball.

After leaving college, Sting worked as a personal fitness trainer and competed in bodybuilding ...until the night that changed his life.

Sting stands 6'3" tall and weighs 252 pounds.

The jam-packed arena and the buzz of the crowd convinced Sting that professional wrestling was the right career move.

One fateful night in 1985, Sting went to the Sports Arena in Los Angeles to watch the legendary wrestler Hulk Hogan in action.

"The crowd was in a frenzy," Sting recalls. "I remember thinking, *something big is going on here.* Then I pictured myself in front of thousands of fans, and I knew that wrestling was for me."

Arena
The WCW spectacle tours the US, attracting huge crowds wherever it goes. WCW employs four two-person crews who travel the country, setting up each arena. Each travel crew is assisted by four helpers.

Many faces

Over the years, Sting's look has changed. When he started as a professional wrestler in 1985, he arrived with a "surfer" look. His hair was dyed blond and his face was covered with colorful face paint. He also wore brightly colored tights.

In October 1996, Sting changed. He started to wear black and white face makeup. He wore a black costume and a long black trenchcoat.

Face paints
Sting designed his first makeup patterns by himself. Nowadays, a costume designer helps him come up with the ghost-like creations.

The bright face paint of the early years

Sting's personality also changed. For over a year, he hardly spoke. He was aloof and mysterious.

Then, in June 1998, Sting joined the Wolfpac. He wore red and black face paint (the official Wolfpac colors). He grew his hair longer and he began to give interviews again.

The red paints didn't last long. Sting was soon in black and white again.

The Wolfpac
The renegade group of wrestlers known as the Wolfpac consisted of Kevin Nash (*above*), Lex Luger, Randy Savage, and Konnan.

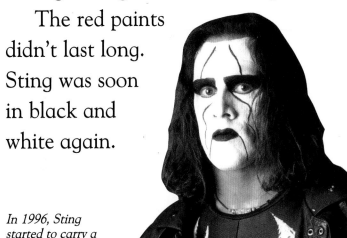

In 1996, Sting started to carry a black baseball bat. It added to his dark mystery.

Sting inflicts the Stinger Splash on Booker T.

Scorpion Death Drop
Sting doesn't use this move often—it's far too dangerous. The Death Drop lands an opponent on his head, and can knock a man out.

Signature moves

Sting has brought the skills that made him a great basketball player into his wrestling style. His athletic, energetic, finishing moves really wow the WCW fans.

Sting's leaping ability lies behind the Stinger Splash. First, he slams an opponent into a corner. Then, after a running start, Sting launches himself into the air, from the center of the ring, crashing into his victim.

He tends to repeat this move several times. It sets him up for his devastating Scorpion Deathlock.

In the Scorpion Deathlock, Sting locks legs with his opponent. He flips his victim onto his stomach, and sits on his lower back. He then pulls his victim's legs up toward the ceiling.

Match over!

Sting wins!

Scorpion Deathlock
This move is practically inescapable. It has been used to defeat such powerful opponents as Hulk Hogan, Randy Savage, and Ric Flair.

Lex Luger struggles as Sting applies the Scorpion Deathlock.

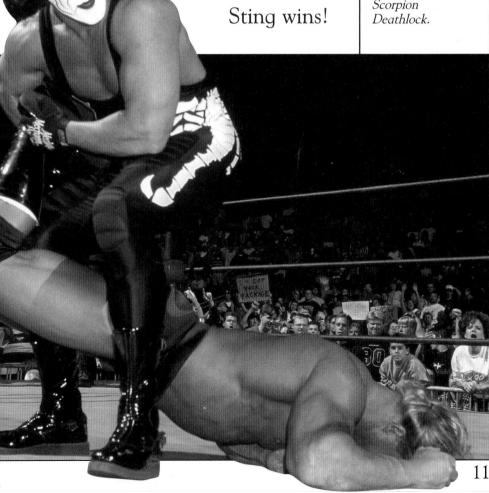

Flash Borden
Before settling on the name Sting, Steve Borden's wrestling name was Flash.

Rick Steiner
Steiner became a wrestler right after he left college, in 1983. He is one of the sports' major figures.

The early years

In the early 1980s, Sting worked as a trainer at Gold's Gym in Venice, California, and also took part in bodybuilding competitions.

After seeing Hulk Hogan wrestle in 1985, Sting teamed up with the Ultimate Warrior, who trained in the same gym. They formed a tag team and began wrestling in California's independent scene, joining the Universal Wrestling Federation (UWF).

When the Ultimate Warrior left the UWF, Sting teamed with Eddie Gilbert, and then Rick Steiner, winning UWF tag team titles with both wrestlers.

In 1987, Sting jumped over to the National Wrestling Alliance (NWA), which became WCW in 1988.

There, he tied with Lex Luger in
a US championship match.

Over the next three years,
Sting steadily worked his way up
the ranks of WCW. He defeated
mid-ranked wrestlers as well as some
top-ranked opponents.

But what Sting was truly hoping
for was a shot at Ric Flair, the WCW
World Heavyweight Champion.

Mr. USA
Sting came
within one
point of
qualifying for
the Mr. USA
bodybuilding
finals in 1984.
His incredible
build prepared
him for his
leap into pro
wrestling the
following year.

Champion at last

On February 6, 1990, Sting was betrayed in the ring by wrestlers he trusted. Worse, he suffered a serious injury to his knee. It looked as if the great man would be out of wrestling for a long, long time.

But less than six months later, at The Great American Bash on July 7, 1990, Sting was back—and he was ready to try for the World Heavyweight Championship.

The odds were stacked against him. He had just come back to the ring from a serious injury. And he was up against Ric Flair, whom many people consider to be the greatest wrestler of all time.

The two wrestlers had met a number of times before, and had formed an intense rivalry.

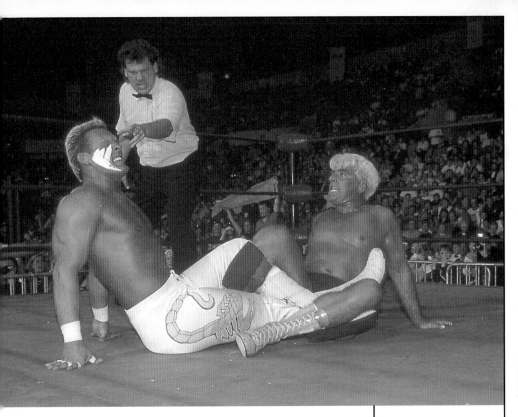

Most wrestling fans thought the match would be a cinch for Flair. But Sting was determined to win wrestling's greatest prize.

It was an epic battle. At one point, Flair got Sting in a Figure Four leg lock—one of wrestling's toughest holds. But Sting wasn't beaten. He struggled free.

He turned his Scorpion Deathlock on Flair, and captured his first world championship.

Sting and Ric Flair lock legs.

After his victory, Sting praised Ric Flair as wrestling's greatest-ever World Champion.

New kid on the mike
Announcer Scott Hudson is the newest member of the WCW broadcast team. He hosts the Saturday night programs.

Sting agreed to a rematch with Ric Flair on January 11, 1991. It was another toughly fought contest. In the end, Flair placed his feet up on the ropes for leverage and pinned Sting to win back the World Championship belt.

On February 29, 1992, Sting took on Lex Luger in an attempt to regain the world championship.

OOF! Big Van Vader groans in pain as Sting stomps on his foot. Vader certainly gets to feel the Sting!

Sting and Luger had been friends, but when Luger turned on Sting, it led to this revenge-fueled battle. Sting won the fight—and the title.

But in July 1992, Sting lost the championship once more, this time to the wrestler called Big Van Vader. Sting beat Vader in March 1993, and reclaimed the belt—then, six days later, he lost it to Vader again!

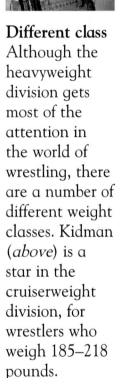

Different class
Although the heavyweight division gets most of the attention in the world of wrestling, there are a number of different weight classes. Kidman (*above*) is a star in the cruiserweight division, for wrestlers who weigh 185–218 pounds.

Tell it like it is
Since the early 1990s, Tony Schiavone has been the voice of WCW.

The WCW Heavyweight Championship belt is rumored to be made of solid gold!

It was over a year before Sting regained the world title, when he beat Rick Rude on April 17, 1994. One month later, during a rematch in Japan, Rude defeated Sting— but was then disqualified for hitting Sting with the championship belt.

WCW declared that Sting could still hold the title, but he refused it. He didn't want a title that he hadn't won outright, so the championship was left vacant.

Sting did not win the belt again until February 22, 1998, when he beat Hulk Hogan. Sting stayed champion until April, when he lost the title to Randy Savage. Sting's next reign as WCW Heavyweight Champion was a real recordbreaker— it was the shortest in wrestling history!

He beat Diamond Dallas Page for the title on April 26, 1999, at 9pm. Two hours later, Page won the title back!

On the air
The spectacle of WCW wrestling has kept fans glued to their TV screens since 1985, when ESPN began broadcasting a weekly show.

No manners: Sting faces Rick Rude in 1994.

The Professor
Fans call WCW announcer Mike Tenay "The Professor" because of his vast knowledge of wrestling around the world.

Bash at the Beach
WCW stages 12 spectacular pay-per-view events each year, including Bash at the Beach, held every July.

Facing the nWo

At Bash at the Beach 1996, Sting teamed up with Lex Luger and Randy Savage in a three-man tag team. Their rivals were Kevin Nash, Scott Hall, and Hulk Hogan.

But this was no straightforward encounter. Nash, Hall, and Hogan used the occasion to announce they had formed the nWo (New World Order), and were planning to take over WCW.

Things got even worse. Sting's team—the good guys—lost to the renegades. The nWo had begun a reign of terror over WCW.

After this, Sting vowed to do whatever he could to stop the attempted takeover.

Sting and Randy Savage face the media.

Savage stands 6'1" tall, and weighs 250 lbs.

Bull rope
There are many strange sights in wrestling—one of the strangest is the bull rope match, where two wrestlers are tied to each other by a 10-foot rope!

Mean Gene
Longtime wrestling personality Gene Okerlund is nicknamed "Mean Gene." This WCW announcer has set the standard for wrestling journalism.

Fake!

At Fall Brawl 1996, Sting and Luger were supposed to team up with Ric Flair and Arn Anderson. "Team WCW" vowed to challenge the nWo again. But a week before Fall Brawl, Sting attacked Luger!

Or so it seemed. Could Sting really have turned against his teammate? And why would he do such a thing?

On the day of the scheduled match, Team WCW was a mess.

Sting's teammates turned on him. They were furious with him for betraying them.

Then, who should show up but Sting—the *real* Sting! Someone had put on his face paint and costume and pretended to be him! Sting disposed of the impostor with ease. Then he started to pummel the nWo.

But suddenly he left the ring. "You finish them off," he said to his teammates as he walked away.

Without Sting's help, the nWo defeated Team WCW.

No one knows why Sting left his teammates when they needed him most. Some people think that he was angry with them because they had believed that he would betray them.

Only one thing is for certain: from then on, Sting changed. He became a totally different kind of wrestler, with a whole new attitude and a whole new look.

Monday Nitro
Sting regularly appears on Monday Nitro, the popular WCW program which has been shown on cable TV since 1995.

Superstition
Sting has a superstitious prematch ritual. "I slap each kneepad after I put it on," he tells us.

Partners
Sting's all-time
favorite tag
team partner is
Rick Steiner.

*This graveyard
setting provides an
eerie backdrop to
Halloween Havoc.*

Mystery man

Following the "fake Sting" incident,
the real Sting disappeared for
a few weeks. When he returned,
in October 1996, his look had
totally changed. His blond hair and
colorful face paint had been replaced
by dark locks and ghostlike face
paint. He dressed all in black.

His personality had changed, too.
He grew silent and sullen, and
quickly became the mystery
man of WCW.

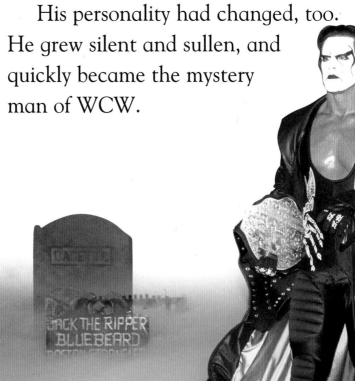

Sting would appear unexpectedly in the rafters of an arena, watching as matches took place below. Sometimes, when the nWo got too powerful, or thought they were unbeatable, Sting would drop down from his perch above and stomp the villains like a dark avenger.

Bobby Heenan
Bobby "The Brain" Heenan has been involved in wrestling for 35 years! He's been a wrestler and a manager, and is now a TV announcer.

Fake Sting
At one point, the fake Sting dared to return to the ring. Real Sting disposed of him in silence, like an angry ghost.

Rebel, rebel Kevin Nash (*above*) split the nWo from within when he broke away to lead the rebel Wolfpac.

Nitro Girls Between matches, these beautiful and talented dancers entertain the crowd. The girls are often caught up in the drama of WCW!

The Wolfpac

As WCW fought to keep the nWo from tearing it apart, a new group emerged. The red and black Wolfpac, led by Kevin Nash, added to WCW's problems. This new faction joined the battle for control of the league.

In May 1997, just as a Monday Nitro was going off the air, the Wolfpac handed Sting one of their red and black T-shirts. They asked him to join them. The world of wrestling held its breath.

In June, the Wolfpac got their answer. Following a tag team match where Nash and Luger faced the Giant and Hogan, Sting dropped from the rafters. He was wearing a black and white nWo T-shirt.

But then Sting turned and knocked Hogan down. He tore off the nWo T-shirt.

Beneath his clothes, Sting wore a Wolfpac T-shirt. The wrestling world had its answer: Sting had joined the Wolfpac!

Once he had joined the Wolfpac, Sting started to wear red and black makeup.

Thriller
The wrestler Sting most enjoys watching in the ring is Rey Mysterio Jr. His athletic, acrobatic style thrills wrestling audiences— and Sting, too!

Big in Japan
Professional wrestling is extremely popular in Japan, where it is called "puroesu."

Goldberg

On September 14, 1998, one of the most anticipated battles in wrestling finally took place. Sting, one of the most interesting and popular wrestlers in WCW, clashed with Goldberg, the WCW World Heavyweight Champion who had never been defeated.

Finished!
To defeat an opponent, Goldberg first "spears" him with a football tackle, before lifting him in the air and slamming him to the mat—the Jackhammer.

Sting hit Goldberg with everything he had. Yet the champ took Sting's best and was still standing.

Finally, Sting got Goldberg in a Scorpion Deathlock. It looked as if Goldberg's long streak of victories might be about to end...

...until Hulk Hogan jumped in the ring! He kicked Sting as Goldberg broke free. The champ slammed Sting with a Spear, then the Jackhammer, and Sting was defeated.

Battle for the presidency

By January 1999, Sting had left the Wolfpac and was once again an aloof, ghostlike warrior. But the mysterious one was still at the center of excitement and controversy.

Old friends
Flair, Anderson, and Vicious (*above*) have been allies since fighting with Barry Windham in the Four Horsemen.

In July 1999, while wrestling legend Ric Flair was president of WCW, Sting challenged Flair to a match. The winner would take the presidency! At Monday Nitro on July 19th, the two met.

Flair had a back injury and Sting dominated the fight. But Flair's buddies made it tough for Sting to close out the victory. Both Arn Anderson and Sid Vicious tried to jump in the ring to help Flair, but Sting disposed of them easily.

Eventually, Sting was declared the winner. The mysterious warrior was president of WCW!

But Sting was not president for long. On August 9th, he resigned. Who knows what the next unexpected move will be for this mysterious warrior? Stay tuned!

Terry Funk
The top position at WCW stayed vacant from August 1999 until January 2000, when Terry Funk took over.

Why did Sting resign?
Sting never really wanted to run WCW, but he saw the July '99 match as one more chance to battle Ric Flair. Putting the presidency on the line added intrigue to the encounter!

Greatest foes

During his long career, Sting has faced the brightest and the best. Now meet the wrestlers he considers his greatest opponents.

Kevin Nash
The wrestler they call "Big Sexy" stands close to seven feet tall and weighs over 300 pounds. His size and agility make him a dangerous foe.

Ric Flair

His glittering robes, breathtaking entrances, and cocky attitude have made him a long-time fan favorite. But Ric "Nature Boy" Flair is a master of power as well as style. He has won 13 world championships and has taken every major title, beating a long list of champions.

Flair's signature moves— the Figure-Four Leg Lock and the Flying Knee Drop—have kept him at the top since the 1970s.

The Total Package

One look tells you why fans call him "The Total Package." The wrestler who was formerly known as Lex Luger has the physique of a world class bodybuilder. This amazing athlete can take down wrestling's biggest bad guys using his signature Torture Rack.

The Total Package has won a WCW World Championship, two WCW tag team titles, and four WCW US belts. He is great friends with Sting and they co-own fitness centers.

The Total Package stands 6'4" tall and weighs around 270 lbs.

Scott Hall
This "bad boy" has clashed with Sting many times. All wrestlers fear his finishing move, the powerful Outsider's Edge.

Rick Steiner

Rick Steiner's wrestling career started at the University of Michigan, where he took fourth place in the NCAA wrestling championships. Once he went pro, Rick became part of one of the greatest tag teams in the history of wrestling, joining his brother Scott.

The Steiner brothers dominated WCW until Scott defected to the renegade nWo, which led to a feud between the two brothers.

Hulk Hogan
He's the most famous wrestler of all time. Since joining WCW in June 1994, Hulk Hogan has earned eight world championship titles.

Scott Steiner

Known as "Big Poppa Pump,"
Scott Steiner claims to have
the biggest arms in WCW—and
who's going to argue with him?
After a great NCAA college
wrestling career, Scott Steiner
joined WCW, teaming up with
his brother Rick.

In 1998, Scott joined the nWo.
Rick Steiner turned his
back on his brother,
and Scott became
one of wrestling's
baddest bad guys.

DDP
Diamond
Dallas Page,
known as DDP,
is a "people's
champion" who
just happens
to have one
of the most
devastating
moves in
wrestling,
the Diamond
Cutter.

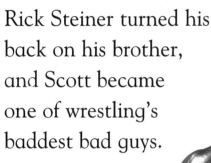

*Scott Steiner is
6'1" tall and
weighs around
235 pounds.*

Bret Hart
Known as Bret "The Hitman" Hart, he is the most famous Canadian wrestler in history. When he's not winning matches with his signature Sharpshooter maneuver, Hart is a columnist and cartoonist for the Calgary Sun newspaper.

Arn Anderson

Anderson is one of the greatest pro wrestlers of all time. He started his career in 1982, and later teamed with his cousin Ole Anderson to form the Minnesota Wrecking Crew, a tag-team sensation.

In the WCW, he won six tag team titles and the TV Championship. Anderson is best known as a member of the Four Horsemen.

Anderson inflicts his devastating signature move, the Spinebuster, on Sting.

Konnan

Konnan's wrestling style combines high flying acrobatics with mat-pounding heavyweight power. Known as K-Dogg, he has won the U.S. Mexican national title and the World Heavyweight Championship.

Born in Cuba and raised in Miami, Konnan was a boxer, fighting for the U.S. Navy Boxing Team before turning his fiery personality and tremendous strength to the wrestling ring.

Sid Vicious
Vicious has torn through the world of wrestling, putting together a winning streak of over 150 matches, second only to Goldberg's 175.

Since the early days of his arrival in WCW (right) Konnan has catured the fans' attention. He is one of the new generation of WCW stars.

Favorite venue
"My favorite
arena to
wrestle in is
the Baltimore
Arena," says
Sting. "I've
had some great
moments
there."

Greatest matches

During a recent interview, Sting was
asked which he considered to be his
greatest contests. He chose three
fights, in no particular order.

One favorite memory was of
Starrcade 1998, when Sting fought
Hulk Hogan. At one point, it seemed
that Hogan had won. However, Bret
Hart protested that the referee had
counted Sting out too quickly.

The match continued, and in the end Sting defeated Hogan with a Scorpion Deathlock to capture his third WCW World Championship.

Sting is also proud of his victory against Ric Flair at the 1990 Great American Bash. That day, he won his first world championship.

Finally, Sting recalled the first Clash of Champions in 1988, also against Ric Flair. In this tremendous struggle, the two men battled for 45 minutes—without a winner.

Archrival "Hacksaw" Jim Duggan is Sting's arch-rival—at the card table! Both wrestlers enjoy playing card games.

Sting and Ric Flair have a long history.

Staying fit

For Sting, fitness has always been a way of life. Before he became a wrestler, he was a personal trainer and bodybuilder. Sting and fellow WCW superstar The Total Package have owned gyms together for many years. Sting still follows a routine of weightlifting to strengthen both his upper body and his legs.

"I'm in the gym four days a week," Sting explains. "It's the only way to stay in this kind of shape. A few years ago I got really out of shape, and that just wasn't a good thing for me, as a wrestler or in life."

As well as lifting weights on a regular basis, Sting runs, swims, or cycles three or four days a week. These are all cardiovascular activities, which means they help build up strength and endurance, and strengthen the heart, too.

Bad habits!
Although Sting knows the value of eating a healthy diet, very rarely he treats himself to cookies, pizza, or pralines-and-cream ice cream!

Weights
Sting advises beginners to weightlifting to always work with a spotter. It's safer in case you lose control of the weights.

Step-by-step
As weightlifters get stronger, they gradually start lifting heavier and heavier weights.

In 1990, Sting was injured when he tore a tendon in his knee. Tendons hold muscle and bone together. They take a long time to heal.

This conditioning is important for general health. It also helps Sting when he enters the ring.

Sting has worked very hard, both in and out of the ring, to reach the top of his profession. And he knows he must spend many hours in the gym to stay at the top. "Pumping iron" (lifting weights) and running on the treadmill help him to avoid injury, increase his strength and flexibility, and keep his weight at its ideal level.

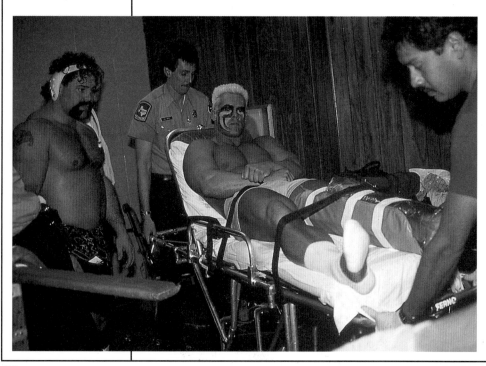

To help protect his injured knee, Sting had to strengthen the knee muscles. He spent hours in the gym performing special strengthening exercises.

"So many of the guys I fight are bigger than me. Some weigh in at 280 or even 300 pounds," Sting explains.

"I like to keep myself around 250 pounds, so I need to rely on energy and athleticism to win my matches. In order to maintain that kind of wrestling style, I've got to be in top cardiovascular condition."

Injury
After his injury, Sting did strengthening exercises to build up the leg muscles. These included leg extensions to build up his quadriceps (top of the thigh) and leg curls to strengthen his hamstrings (underside of the thigh).

On screen

Sting's first movie appearance came in the 1998 film *The Real Reason (Men Commit Crimes.)* He played a character called Sparkie. He also appeared in the wrestling movie *Ready To Rumble.* And recently, he starred in a TV movie called *Shutterspeed*, where he played an undercover cop named Riley Davis.

"I enjoyed every moment of making the movie," Sting says. "Acting is something I could spend the rest of my life doing, if I could be so lucky."

Sting worked on the film for two months, shooting in Vancouver, British Columbia.

"I love performing," he admits. "It's not as physically demanding or tough on my body as wrestling."

Sting took acting classes for nine months before stepping in front of the cameras for the first time.

Sting is married, and he and his wife have four children.
As a father, he knows how important it is to be a good role model to his young fans. His behavior in and outside the ring shows how seriously he takes that responsibility.

Giving something back

Out of the ring, Sting's most fulfilling work is with the Make-A-Wish Foundation and the Starlight Foundation. Sting devotes many hours of his free time to these charities, which exist to grant wishes to very ill children.

Sting loves meeting with the children themselves. "I meet a lot of youngsters who maybe haven't smiled for months, because of illness and difficult treatments," he explains.

Sting meets some of his many fans

Beam me up!
Once, Sting couldn't make it to Florida from his home in California to visit a sick child. So he set up a satellite broadcast, which beamed him right into the child's room!

Thankful
"It can be heartbreaking, knowing that you are speaking with children who may not make it," Sting says of his charity work. "I'm thankful to be able to add something to their lives."

"It's nice to be able to put a smile on their faces. That's the most meaningful, rewarding part of being a celebrity."

Sting knows there's more to being a champion than just winning matches. He respects his fans. That's why his popularity has lasted so long—and why the fans know he'll stay at the top for years to come!

Glossary

Anticipated
Something that people look forward to.

Attitude
The way a person views a situation or behaves towards another person.

Avenger
Someone who punishes another, in return for a wrong that person has done.

Cardiovascular
To do with the heart and blood.

Columnist
A person who writes a regular feature for newspapers or magazines.

Consecutive
Following one after another, with no breaks or interruption.

Disqualified
Counted out of a contest or game for breaking the rules.

Demolish
To completely break down or destroy.

Devastating
A very powerful and destructive force.

Dominated
Was completely in charge or in control.

Eerie
Mysterious and ghostly; spooky.

Faction
A number of people, forming a group within a bigger organization.

Feud
A long-running fight or quarrel between two or more people.

Finishing move
In wrestling, the standard move which a wrestler uses to defeat his opponent and end a match, and for which he is usually known. Also known as a Signature move.

Inevitable
Something that seems destined to happen.

Leverage
Use of a lever to increase power.

Mythic
Legendary.

Opponent
Someone who belongs to the oppposing side of a group or team.

Physique
General appearance and condition of a body.

Pin
In wrestling, to hold an opponent's shoulders to the mat for a count of three. This results in winning the match.

Rafters
A support beam beneath the roof of a building.

Reclaim
To take back something that once belonged to you.

Renegade
Outlaw; a person or group who breaks the rules.

Rivalry
Being in competition with another person.

Signature move
See Finishing move.

Tag team
Usually, a team of two wrestlers. During a tag team match, wrestlers from each side take turns wrestling or resting.

Titanic
Either having or needing great strengh.

Vacant
Empty, unoccupied